Poems for the Seasons

Chosen by Brian Moses

Illustrated by Ellie Jenkins

WINDMILL
BOOKS

Published in 2018 by Windmill Books, an Imprint of Rosen Publishing
29 East 21st Street, New York, NY 10010

Editor: Victoria Brooker
Designer: Lisa Peacock

Acknowledgments: The Compiler and Publisher would like to thank the authors for allowing their poems to
appear in this anthology of poems. Poems © the authors. While every attempt has been made to gain permissions
and provide an up-to-date biography, in some cases this has not been possible and we apologize for any omissions.
Should there be any inadvertent omission, please apply to the Publisher for rectification.

"Snow Joke" was first published in "Funny Poems for Christmas" compiled by Paul Cookson (Scholastic 2006)

Cataloging-in-Publication Data
Names: Moses, Brian.
Title: Poems for the seasons / compiled by Brian Moses.
Description: New York : Windmill Books, 2018. | Series: Poems just for me | Includes index.
Identifiers: ISBN 9781499483918 (pbk.) | ISBN 9781499483871 (library bound) | ISBN 9781508193142 (6 pack)
Subjects: LCSH: Seasons--Juvenile poetry. | Children's poetry, American. | Children's poetry, English.
Classification: LCC PS595.S42 P64 2018 | DDC 811.008'033--dc23

Manufactured in the China
CPSIA Compliance Information: Batch #BS17WM: For Further Information contact Rosen Publishing, New York, New York at 1-800-237-9932

Contents

Spring Phoned

Yesterday
spring phoned to say
it was on its way.

It left
a chirpy message
on nature's answering machine.

And as I lie in bed today
I hear the birds playing the message
over and over again.

Ian Souter

4

Spring

Spring's the time for daffodils
And catkins flippy-floppy,
Woolly lambs and fluffy chicks,
And rabbits hippy-hoppy.

Spring's the time for sunny days,
When sparrows flitter-flutter,
Splishy-splashy rainy days
And puddles in the gutter.

Clare Bevan

Springtime in Bluebell Wood

A million leaves
on trees so tall.
You'll hear birds sing
and cuckoos call
    in Bluebell Wood.

See butterflies,
hear pigeons coo.
The long grass is
still wet with dew
    in Bluebell Wood.

Look! Ferns unfurl,
and green frogs leap.
Brown rabbits hop
and beetles creep
        in Bluebell Wood.

A fence to climb.
A sunny day.
Just stand and watch
the bluebells sway
        in Bluebell Wood.

Wes Magee

Spring in the City

Spring has come to the city,
to the streets and the railway line.
Winter is packing its bags,
the sun has begun to shine.

The cherry tree in our garden
wears a wedding dress of white.
Geese are in flight once more
and days are warm with delight.

There are plenty of baby lambs
to see at the city farm,
and a single primrose shows its head
at the dump, like a lucky charm.

A heron is raising its young
at the flooded gravel pits,
and the nest box on our garden wall
is a shelter for baby chicks.

Wrens are finding new homes
in an untidy, overgrown hedge.
Pigeons choose a tall building
and jostle for space on a ledge.

Spring has come to the city,
there's a lightness in everyone's tread.
Office workers have shed their coats,
there's a promise of summer ahead.

Brian Moses

What Is Summer For?

Summer is for sunhats,
for sandals or bare feet.
Summer is for sunshades,
to shelter from the heat.

Summer is for picnics
and playing in the park.
Summer is for staying out
all day long till dark!

Kate Williams

Summer Clouds

Clouds are drifts of soft white flowers
strewn across a placid blue lake.

Clouds are slow white jellyfish
floating in a clear blue ocean.

Clouds are angry black panthers
crouched, snarling, over the hills.

Clouds are thundering black horses
rearing and tossing their stormy heads.

Penny Kent

Bed in Summer

In winter I get up at night
And dress by yellow candle-light.
In summer, quite the other way,
I have to go to bed by day.

I have to go to bed and see
The birds still hopping on the tree,
Or hear the grown-up people's feet
Still going past me in the street.

And does it not seem hard to you,
When all the sky is clear and blue,
And I should like so much to play,
To have to go to bed by day?

R. L. Stevenson

Dear Summer

Dear Summer, you're always my favorite.
I really do like you a lot.
You come every year,
and I'm glad when you're here.
I don't even mind that you're hot.

Dear Summer, whenever you visit,
I love to go outside to play.
I get to wear shorts
and play summertime sports,
or sometimes do nothing all day.

I put on my goggles and swim suit,
and head for the beach or the park.
I go for a hike
or I ride on my bike,
and stay awake long after dark.

Dear Summer, I'm glad you could join us.
Without you, it won't be the same.
I promise I know
that you do have to go,
but, still, it seems sort of a shame.

I'm sure that I'm going to miss you.
The school year is finally here.
I had so much fun
playing out in the sun.
I guess that I'll see you next year.

Kenn Nesbitt

The Swallow

Fly away, fly away, over the sea,
    Sun-loving swallow, for summer is done.
Come again, come again, come back to me,
    Bringing the summer and bringing the sun.

Christina Rossetti

Autumn?

Some people call it "Autumn"
Some people call it "Fall"
I call it "Damp Dark Squelch Time"
As I don't like it at all.

Chris White

Autumn Song

There's a chill in the air
that wasn't there
just over a month ago.

There's a dew on the grass
each morning I pass
the field where the stream runs slow.

People gathering hops,
farmers harvesting crops,
the countryside all of a bustle:

the stubble is burning,
the tractors are churning
and at night the leaves eerily rustle.

Ripe apples are falling,
lonely church bells are calling,
over orchards they sullenly ring.

The summer plants wilt
and my bed gets a quilt,
how I wish I could sleep until spring.

John Rice

Autumn Action Rhyme

Here are the trees
so leafy and tall.

*(Stand with arms up as branches,
    hands and fingers extended)*

Look at the leaves
as they shrivel and fall.

*(Curl up hands, then use them to show
    leaves falling down toward ground)*

Listen and hear
what a whispery sound

*(Place hand up to ear to suggest listening.
    Some children can make whispery noises too.)*

they make as they flutter
and float to the ground.

*(Bring leaf-hands down to rest on
    floor for brief pause.)*

Here are the branches,
so naked and plain

*(Stand and extend arms again, this time with
    fists closed and arms slightly drawn in.)*

waiting for Spring
when the leaves grow again.

*(Open hands to show fingers stretching out.
    Push arms out a little to emphasize gesture.)*

Tony Mitton

Sounds Like Winter

Winter is CRUNCH!
Snow underfoot
Winter is SNIP!
Wrapping paper is cut
Winter is WHOOSH!
Cold winds blow
Winter is GIGGLE!
Play in the snow
Winter is LA LAAAA!
Carol-singing group
Winter is SLURP!
Drinking hot soup
Winter is MMMMMM!
Give the pudding a stir
But above all else
Winter is BRRRRRRRRRRRR!

Chris White

I Hear Thunder (With Actions in Parentheses)

I hear thunder, I hear thunder.
   (Stamp feet on floor.)
Hark, don't you? Hark, don't you?
   (Put hand to ear.)
Pitter-patter raindrops,
   (Move hand down slowly, waggling fingers.)
Pitter-patter raindrops,
I'm wet through —
   (Shake body.)
You are too.
   (Point to someone else.)

Anon

December

December, December,
A month to remember,
A month full of darkness and light,
A month full of rushing
And sharing and hoping.
A month full of one special night.

Daphne Kitching

Mr. Snowman

Monday built our Snowman
Sitting proud and fat
Tuesday gave him a football scarf
And the warmest woolly hat
Wednesday gave him his button eyes
Thursday a carrot nose
Friday gave him sticks for arms
And Saturday more clothes
But Sunday gave bad weather
The sky began to cry
Sunday took our snowman
We never said goodbye.

Debra Bertulis

Snow Joke

Why does it have to be Snowmen?
Why is it never Snowgirls?
Why can't we build a Snow-Princess
With berries for rubies and pearls?
Why can't we pick her some holly
And give her a spiky, green crown?
What about icicle diamonds
To wear on her glittery gown?
What about crowds of Snow Ladies
With twiggy and twizzly curls?
Why does it have to be Snowmen?
Why is it NEVER Snowgirls?

Clare Bevan

The Seasons in Me

I can be sunny,
I can be warm,
I can blow hot and cold,
I can thunder and storm.

I can be breezy,
I can be bright.
I can be dark
I can be light.

I can be wet,
I can be dry,
I can change like the seasons
in the blink of an eye.

From the outside
can anyone see
that inside I have
all the seasons in me?

Jane Clarke

Time

Seconds to minutes
And hours into days,
The gleam of the Moon
And the Sun's golden rays,
Through weeks, months, and years
The clocks tick and chime
As they show, the World over,
The passing of Time!

Dandelions, sun dials,
The clock in the hall,
A wristwatch, Big Ben,
Clocks great and clocks small.
They all show how Time
Is unwilling to stay —
And how quickly Tomorrow
Turns into Today!

Trevor Harvey

Further information

Websites

For web resources related to the subject of this book, go to: **www.windmillbooks.com/weblinks** and select this book's title.

About the Poets:

Debra Bertulis' life-long passion is the written and spoken word, and she is the author of many published poems for children. She is regularly invited to schools where her workshops inspire pupils to compose and perform their own poetry. Debra lives in Herefordshire, England, where she enjoys walking the nearby Welsh hills and seeking out second-hand book shops!

Clare Bevan used to be a teacher until she decided to become a writer instead. So far, she has written stories, plays, song lyrics, picture books, and a huge heap of poetry. Her poems have appeared in over one hundred anthologies, and she loves performing them in schools. Her hobbies are reading and acting, and she once dressed up as a farmyard chicken.

Jane Clarke is the author of over 80 children's books including the award-winning picture books *Stuck in the Mud*, illustrated by Gary Parsons, and *Gilbert the Great*, illustrated by Charles Fuge. She's delighted to have a poem in this anthology.

Trevor Harvey's humorous poems for children have now been included in around 200 anthologies and publications. He has also written one-act plays for amateur dramatic groups and has been a judge of play competitions for The Sussex Playwrights' Club and for New Writing South.

Daphne Kitching lives in East Yorkshire, England, with her husband. She is a former primary school teacher and specialist teacher of pupils with SpLD (Dyslexia), a poet, a pyrographer, and a priest in a lively East Riding parish. She loves ladybugs, long walks, learning to knit, and keeping up with all her children and grandchildren.

Wes Magee: *Deep in the Green Wood* and *Here Come the Creatures* are two of Wes Magee's recent books for children. He lives in a tiny village on the Yorkshire Wolds, England, and has a pet dog, a golden retriever called Maya.

Tony Mitton has been published as a poet for children since the early '90s. He has also written many successful verse picture books and works blending poetry with narrative. He has won several awards. He lives in Cambridge, England, where he continues to read and write.

30

Brian Moses lives in Burwash, England, where the famous writer Rudyard Kipling once lived. He travels the country performing his poetry and percussion show in schools, libraries and theaters. He has published over 200 books including the series of picture books *Dinosaurs Have Feelings Too.*

Kenn Nesbitt is a children's poet. In 2013, he was named Children's Poet Laureate by the Poetry Foundation. He has written many books, including *When the Teacher Isn't Looking and Other Funny Poems About School,* and *The Biggest Burp Ever: Funny Poems for Kids.*

John Rice has published seven collections of poetry for children and his poems have appeared in over 300 anthologies, magazines, and newspapers. Several of his poems have been broadcast by the BBC, and some have been set to music. He was Glasgow's Poet-in-Residence for two years during the Robert Burns 250th anniversary celebrations. He lives in Cumbria, England, and regularly visits schools in the north of England and southern Scotland.

Christina Rossetti (1830-94) was an English poet who published a number of books and rhymes for young children, including *Sing Song* and *Goblin Market*— a fairy story in verse.

Ian Souter is retired from teaching and loves to exercise, play music, and travel. He lives in the wilds of Surrey, England, but also loves to visit, in particular, France and Australia. On his travels he also keeps an eye (and an ear) open for words and ideas.

Sometimes he finds them hanging from trees or people's mouths or even sparkling in the sunshine.

R.L. Stevenson (1850-94) was a Scottish author and poet. His best-known books are *Treasure Island* and *Kidnapped.* His collection, *A Child's Garden of Verses,* is a classic of children's poetry.

Chris White has written many poetry books, including *Don't Put Dave in the Microwave!* and a book of stories including "Stumpy's Big Adventure." He illustrates his own work and other writers' works, too. Chris has taken his poetry performances around the world to places such as China, Dubai, and Congo!

Kate Williams When Kate's children were young, she made up poems to read them at bedtime. It was their clever idea that she send them off to a publisher, and she's been contributing to children's anthologies ever since! Kate finds writing a poem is like making a collage, but less sticky—except that she's stuck in the craze! She provides workshops for schools, too.

Index of first lines